MAGIC IS INSIDE THE CRYSTAL

I HOPE YOU'RE NOT AFRAID OF SPIRITS

NEETA RAVARIYA

Made with ❤ on the Notion Press Platform
www.notionpress.com

Contents

Preface

The story is about a magic object called Crystal pot which fulfills everyone's wishes. After the death of a Queen she handed over the Crystal Pot to her daughter, but it got stolen by a person. After stealing it, that person killed the Queen's daughter. Then after so many years that girl came again in a modern era. Did she remember anything? Would she take revenge? Or She would forgive him. Read this amazing novel to know what happened next. By the way, the ending will shock you.

The story is full of mystery and secrets. Readers will find all the flavours in just one story.

CHAPTER ONE

Abandoned house

There was one group of five friends. The group consisted of Marietta, Sia, Jenny, Sid and Samar.They always supported each other. They all lived in the same area. Sia was very humble amongst all. Marietta was a quiet girl but smart too. Jenny and Samar were naughty and Sid was the smartest one. All were incomplete without each other just like Best Friends Forever.

One day, it wasSia's birthday. Sia invited her friends to her birthday party. Jenny and Sid had already arrived at the party. Marietta and Samar had not bought any gift yet. Therefore, they both decided to buy a gift for her. They both walked their way, because the shop was not so far from Sia's birthday place. When they were going, suddenly on the way, Marietta's gaze went on one house and she stopped there. That house looked so scary, As if no one had lived there for a long time. She was constantly staring at the house. While Samar was walking, he realised that Marietta was not walking with him. He turned around and looked at Marietta and thought,

'What is she looking at there?' and he went to her,

"What happened?" Samar asked.

"Samar, do you know anything about this house?" Marietta asked him.

Samar asked curiously, "What...! What about this house? I don't know anything."

"This isn't a normal house. This is an abandoned house." Marietta said with a grimace.

Bemused, Samar asked again, "What do you mean?"

"Once I had read in the newspaper about this house. This is a haunted house. One woman was living here and one day she was found dead in her house. It seemed like someone had killed her brutally. After her death, for 3 years no one even went around this house. Then exactly after 3 years, one couple came here to stay. Their names were Mr. And Mrs. Shawy. However, they did not stay here long. In just 2 days they left." Marietta revealed the story. Samar was astonished to hear all this and he was not ready to believe.

"Then, What happened? Why did Mr. And Mrs. Shawy leave this house?" Samar asked.

Marietta replied, "Many people asked the same question. So, Mr. Shawy said he had heard someone screaming and making weird voices."

"Oh! That's scary!" Samar murmured.

"You know, Samar? I'm getting such weird vibes that something is going to happen with us. Something strange is happening to me right now. I don't know what it is? But it's weird." Marietta said. Marietta was getting an intuition about something.

"It's not safe to stay here. We are getting late. Let's go."Samar said and grabbed her hand and started walking away.

Then suddenly one kind of sound came, "cheeeuuu..." as if someone had opened the gate. Marietta heard the voice, stopped again and looked back.

"Samar, did you hear that sound?" She said hurriedly.

"No, I heard no sound. Let's go now. Sia must be waiting for us." Samar said and he sounded irritated.

Marietta thought that, 'This may be my illusion.' Then they both left from there. However, it was not her illusion. Gate had actually been opened by someone. Then they both arrived at the party. They all were celebrating Sia's birthday.

"Tell me Sia, what do you want for your birthday gift?" Sid wished her and asked.

"I only want my friends to be with me forever, nothing else I want." Sia smiled and said.

"We all will stay together forever." They said together. "We won't leave you, Sia. Not even in the grave." Samar added. Everyone laughed happily. Then they wrapped up the party and they all set to go home.

CHAPTER TWO

The Mysterious girl

The party ended at midnight. The group was going home. The path to their homes passed by the side of the haunted house. While Sid was driving, Suddenly his gaze fell on one girl. That girl was standing exactly next to the haunted house. She was gesturing as if she wanted a lift.

"Hey guys, look at that girl. I think she needs help." Sid said.

That was a dark night. Samar and Marietta knew that this was a haunted place. Therefore, Marietta tapped her hand twice on Sid's shoulder and she said hurriedly.

"Don't stop the car, Sid. It's not safe to stop the car at midnight."

"What are you saying, Marietta? She is alone at this time. We should help her." Sid said.

Sid stopped the car Instead of agreeing to Marietta. Then he looked at that girl. For a moment his eyes stuck on her, he froze for a few moments. That girl was looking so beautiful. She had worn a Red gown and kept her long hair open. It seemed as if an angel came down to the ground.

"Hello, Will you please drop me to the highway? Because it's difficult to find any lift here and I'm in a hurry." That girl said politely in her beautiful voice.

Sid suddenly flared up and said excitedly. "Of course, why not? We will drop you. Come, sit in the car."

Samar and Marietta looked at each other. Sia and Jenny were also impressed with her beauty and gesture.

After a few minutes Samar asked that unknown girl' "Hey, What's your name?"

"My name is Ruhi." She replied.

"So, what are you doing here alone, at this time?" Marietta asked suspiciously.

Ruhi stayed quiet. She started moving her eyeballs as if she was hiding something. She was going to say something like, "I...I..."

"Oh come on, why are you both interrogating her? She might have some work." Sid interrupted, as he realised that she did not want to tell them. Then Ruhi smiled at Sid.

"By the way, I'm going to my cousin's home. She is not well and she had called me to come, that's why." Ruhi said to them.

Later, the highway came and she said to stop the car. Sid stopped and she stepped out from the car and turned around to Sid. She gave a little smile and she waved her hand towards everyone.

"Bye Ruhi, see you soon." Sid said to her with excitement.

"We'll definitely meet, Sid." Ruhi said. Then she turned back and walked her way.

The next day Sid was going somewhere. He was going from the same road he had used last night. He again saw Ruhi at the same place where he had seen her last night. He stopped the car in front of her and asked her,

"Ruhi! What are you doing here again?"

"I was waiting for you Sid." Ruhi replied.

"For me?" Sid was surprised. "But how did you know that I will come here?"

"I just felt like that." Ruhi said.

"Oh! I think you need a lift again. Am I right?" He said.

"Yaa, that's true. Will you...?" she asked.

"Oh come on Ruhi, Of course I will drop you. Come sit. By the way, where do you want to go?" He asked her.

She said, "Just drop me at BG's Restaurant."

"Oh great, even I'm going to the same restaurant and my friends are also coming there. I will surprise them." Sid said.

Ruhi sat in the car. Later, they both reached the restaurant. They both entered and went to the table where Sid's friends sat.

"Look here guys, who came with me?" Sid said.

After seeing Ruhi with Sid, everyone was surprised, "Ruhi! What are you doing here?" Marietta asked surprisingly.

"I'm here to meet my cousin. She is on the way." Ruhi said.

"Is she the same girl you were going for at midnight?" Jenny asked.

"Yes, she is the same girl. My cousin Sahara." Ruhi replied.

While they were all talking with Ruhi, Sahara came in the restaurant and loudly took Ruhi's name, "Hey Ruhi..." she came towards Ruhi and thanked her,

"Thank you so much Ruhi for coming. Whenever I needed any help, you came and helped me. You are such a sweetheart. Even last night you came for my help."Sahara hugged her.

Sid and his friends were also listening to their conversation. After watching this moment, Samar went close to Marietta. He leaned a little towards Marietta and whispered in her ear.

"I think your perception about her is wrong. She was right about last night that she was going to her cousin's home. I think she is not as bad as you think."

"Yes, you're right. She is not so bad but she is not so good as well." Marietta said with a grimace. "Her dark intense eyes are saying everything about her, as if she has a dark secret and she is hiding it." Samar shook his head and took a deep breath.

After that, Ruhi introduced her cousin Sahara to the group and later she said,

"Excuse us guys, you all have fun. We are going to our table." Then, they both shifted to their booked table.

One side Marietta had many questions in her mind, and on the other side, Sid started liking Ruhi. Sid wanted to spend more and more time with her. Ruhi and Sahara were a few tables away from the group.

"Are they the same people you were talking about?" Sahara asked Ruhi.

"Yes." Ruhi replied.

"Are you sure that they will help you? "Sahara asked.

"I'm damn sure. Our first plan worked. They will believe me now. This is the right time to start our next plan. Are you ready?" Ruhi asked.

"Anything for you. I am ready. Let's go." Sahara said confidently.

They both showed thumbs up to each other. Marietta saw them both doing thumbs up to each other. However, Ruhi and Sahara didn't realize that. But, Marietta kept this moment in her mind. Because she knew that if she said this to anyone, no one would believe her.

CHAPTER THREE

Ruhi's real motive

The next day, Sid was going somewhere again. While Sid was driving, he saw one girl lying down in the middle of the road in front of the haunted house. He stopped his car and stepped out of the car. He went close to that girl. That girl's hair was on her face. To see her face, he moved the hair from her face. After seeing her face, he was shocked. That girl was none other than Ruhi and her forehead was bleeding.

"Ruhi, Wake up. What happened? Come on..., wake up." He started yelling.

He tried a lot to wake her up. However, she did not wake up. Later, he lifted her in his arms and put her in the car. He took her to Sia's home. He pressed the doorbell after a little struggle because Ruhi was in his arms, Sia opened the door and she also reacted like Sid.

"Oh my God! What happened to her?" Sia asked curiously to Sid.

"I don't know. I found her unconscious in the middle of the road. Now, only she can tell us, what happened to her?" Sid said.

Sia called her other friends Marietta, Samar and Jenny to come to her house. After some time everyone came to Sia's home. Everybody saw that Ruhi was unconscious and her forehead was bleeding. Everyone was shocked.

"What happened? Why is she in this situation?" Marietta asked.

"We don't know. We have to wait for her to come out from unconsciousness. Let her wake up." Sia said.

Later, a doctor came and checked her; he said that, "Someone has hit her on the forehead. By the way, she'll be fine in some time." and the doctor left.

"Something major has happened." Jenny said.

After a while, Ruhi moved her hand. She was trying to wake up. And, finally she opened her eyes. Everyone sat around her on the bed.She woke up and everyone started asking her at the same time, what happened with her and why she fainted on the ground and her forehead was bleeding as well. Is she fine or not?

"Calm down guys, calm down." Ruhi said loudly. "I'm completely fine now. I am only worried about my Crystal Pot. I must have to bring that back from him." Ruhi said worriedly.

"Wait, one second what do you mean by Crystal Pot?" Samar asked.

"Tell us everything in detail. What is happening? How did you get injured?" Sia asked.

"Ok then. First of all, promise me that you guys will help me to bring my Crystal Pot back." Ruhi said to all and she put her hand forward.

After a little discussion they all agreed. Everyone put their hand on Ruhi's hand and promised her that they will help her.

"Now, come with me. I am taking you all to my home. Because the whole history and mystery of Crystal Pot is there." Ruhi said to everyone.

Everybody went with her. When they all reached the gate of the haunted house Marietta suddenly said, "Stop!" Everyone stopped there, they turned back and looked at her.

Sid asked her, "What happened, Marietta? Why are you stopping us?"

"Is this your house?" Marietta looked at Ruhi and said.

"Yes. This is my house. I know what you are thinking right now." She turned around, she looked at the haunted house with intense eyes, and she said, "According to many people this is a haunted and abandoned house. However, according to me nothing is wrong here. Because, I have been living here for 3 months. I did not find anything terrible. Moreover, what you heard about this house is incomplete, I will tell you the whole real story. Therefore, trust me and come with me."

"How can I trust you? I have read an article about this house. Many people have experienced the presence of spirits in this house." Marietta said.

"Don't worry Marietta. We all are together; if something happens we will face it and fight for it together." Jenny said.

Then everyone followed Ruhi. All entered the gate but Marietta was still standing outside the gate. Samar looked back and he saw that Marietta was still outside the gate. He called her and said,

"Marietta, come inside. Don't worry, we all are here."

She nodded her head and got ready to go inside.

"Oh Universe, Please protect us." Marietta prayed before entering the gate.

Ruhi took everyone in her house, offered them to sit, and said,

"Wait here guys; I'm coming right now." Then she went to her bedroom and took one book in her hand and she came down to the hall. She showed the book to all and said,

"This is the book about Crystal Pot. You will all believe me after reading this book."

Sia took that book in her hand and started reading loudly as everyone could hear. "A long time ago. One woman named Mary was living in her native place named 'Crestaland.' Her father was a king of Crestaland. He was a very kind person. He always stayed ready to help people. He was a great devotee of God. After so many struggles, he had earned a Crystal Pot from God. Crystal Pot was created only for the purpose to help those who are in need. Crystal Pot fulfils the wishes. The king gave that Crystal Pot to her daughter when he was on his deathbed and told her to use this to help people. He said,

"Never let this Crystal Pot go into the wrong hands. Otherwise, that bad person will destroy everything." Mary nodded her head with the crying face and promised her dad that she will use Crystal Pot Properly and she will protect this too.

After the death of the king, she handled everything properly. Few years later she fell ill, perhaps she did not use Crystal Pot to make herself healthy. Because she believed that, 'no one can extend life. Only God has the power to give life and take life. Crystal Pot can only fulfil the wishes. It cannot be someone's saviour.' That is why she decided to hand over this Pot to her daughter. Her daughter was only 7 years old. Though she tried her best to use it properly and protect it as well." And Sia closed the book as the story finished.

Ruhi added, "This is not the end. When Mary's daughter finished her 20th year, she shifted to this city, in this house with the Crystal Pot. Unfortunately, this city proved a curse for her. One dark night, a man came into her house silently and tried to steal the Crystal Pot from her. Unluckily, she was alone. She also tried hard to save the Pot. She was not ready to hand over this Pot in the wrong hand. Moreover, in the midst of this fight the evil man took a knife in his hand and stabbed her in the stomach thrice. He snatched Crystal Pot from her hands and ran away from that house."

"How do you know all these things?" Jenny asked.

"I had heard about this somewhere." Ruhi replied.

"Then why did you call the Crystal Pot as yours?" Marietta asked.

"It...It slipped out of my mouth by mistake." She said hesitantly.

"That's alright. By the way, have you ever seen Crystal Pot? Because you said that you want to bring that Pot back." Samar asked.

"Yes. I have already seen that Crystal Pot. In the early morning I went for a jog. I saw that one man sat on the bench holding the Crystal Pot in his hand. I knew everything about Crystal Pot. And, it was obvious that he stole the Pot from Mary's daughter and murdered her. That is why I went silently towards him and snatched the pot from him and ran away from there. Later he started following me and he took a stone in his hand and hit me. He snatched the Crystal Pot from my hand and ran away. That is why I want to bring The Crystal Pot back from him. Because, he was not using it properly and his bad intentions will destroy everything." Ruhi Said. She was telling a false story.

"Is this the only reason behind getting the Crystal Pot back?" Marietta suspected her and asked.

"No, there is one more reason behind this thing. However, I can't tell you right now. But, I promise you that when the right time comes, I will tell you the whole truth.

Trust me I'm doing nothing wrong. If you wish, you can ask for any one thing from the Crystal Pot when we succeed in getting this CrystalPot back." Ruhi said.

After hearing all this, all remained silent for a while. They all started looking at each other. Then after a little thought Samar looked at everyone and blinked his eyes and said to Ruhi,

"Okay then, we will surely help you. Tell us what the plan is?" Samar believed her and asked for a plan to complete the mission. Later Ruhi presented her plan in front of everyone.

Execution of Ruhi's plan

The next day all gathered at Ruhi's house. Ruhi's cousin also came there. Everyone dressed up as per plan. All wore a mask on their faces because they did not want to be identified by that man.

"Are you guys ready?" Ruhi said.

"Yes." All said at once.

"He will not give that Crystal Pot so easily. We have to steal from him anyhow. Be aware guys. Let's go, it's time to execute our plan." Ruhi said.

After a while, they all reached the man's house. They all saw that one party was running at his home. Luckily, that was a masquerade party. They all entered his house. There were many people in that party so this group of people did not seem unfamiliar to anyone.

"Let's divide guys. Ruhi knows what Crystal Pot looks like. Therefore, Ruhi, Sahara and Sid go and find out where the Crystal Pot is. Sia and Jenny, you both keep your eyes on that man and if you find something wrong then immediately call or message me, Marietta and I will handle that man. Understood?" Samar said to all.

All agreed for what Samar said and they all went to play their part. Marietta and Samar went into a corner and stood up there. Marietta joined her hands, closed her eyes and prayed to the Universe as usual.

"Oh Universe, Please take care of everything and protect us."

Samar looked at her and smiled. Ruhi, Sahara and Sid went into that man's bedroom. They checked his wardrobe, under the mattress, also checked under the bed and many more. However, they got nothing except one small key. The key seemed to belong to a treasure. There was no treasure in the bedroom. Therefore, they ignored the key and put it back from where they had taken it. Later Sahara said to Sid and Ruhi,

"Let's go to another room. We haven't found anything here."

While they were going to another room, Sid and the rest were walking.They entered the second room. Sid took a step forward and suddenly he heard something different. A different sound was coming from each of their footsteps while they were walking and a different sound came when they took this step.

"Stop!" Sid said, "I felt the different sound of my footsteps here. I think something is fishy here. Let's check."

Sid bent down and checked the tile, which was making a different noise. Then he saw one small button on the bare side of the tile. He pressed that button. Suddenly that big tile went down a bit and opened automatically. The trio was surprised. They saw a staircase there.

"Sahara, you stay here. Ruhi and I are going down to check. If you see someone coming, Play the tune of the whistle and let us know." Sid said.

Sahara nodded her head and stood there. Ruhi and Sid went down and they saw a treasure chest that was locked. Then Ruhi suddenly remembered that she had seen a key in the bedroom, which seemed to belong to this treasure. She went upstairs and ran towards the bedroom. She took the key and she came back to the secret place. On the other side Jenny and Sia saw that, that man was going towards his room and that secret door was right next to the bedroom. Immediately Sia gestured to Samar and Marietta and pointed at the man. Samar went to Sia and Jenny and said them both,

"Go and try to stop him. Marietta and I are going to alert Sid. Come on, fast."

Then Jenny and Sia went to that man and tried to keep him engaged in conversation.

"Hello, Mr...?" Jenny tried to ask his name.

"Hi, I'm Mr. Sahir Swang. I'm sorry! But, I didn't recognize you. Who are you?" That man said.

Jenny said, "A...A...My name is Lily and her name is Silly." Sia got angry because Jenny called her Silly. Sia hit her elbow onJenny's waist, "Sorry Mr. Swang, she was just kidding. My name is Riya." Sia said.

They both gave their false names. This is how they both tried to stop him. Until then Samar and Marietta went to their other friends Sid, Sahara and Ruhi. They saw that Sahara was standing in one place and rolling her eyes and head. Samar and Marietta went to her and asked her,

"Why are you standing here and where are Sid and Ruhi?"

"They both are in this secret room and looking for Crystal Pot." Sahara told them. Samar and Marietta looked down to the room.

"But, why are you both here? Is everything fine?" Sahara asked them.

"No, nothing is fine. That man is coming to this side. We have to do something." Marietta said worriedly.

"Oh no!" Sahara said anxiously.

While they were thinking about what to do next, Sia called Samar and said,

"Samar, do something fast. Mr. Swang is coming. We tried so hard to stop him but he left."

"Who is Mr. Swang?" Samar asked.

"That murderer." Sia replied.

"Oh no!" Samar babbled. He hung up the call. "Come on, do something fast. That murderer Mr. Swang is coming here." Samar said to Marietta and Sahara.

Trio heard the sound of footsteps. Then Sahara immediately bent down and closed the door of the secret room. After that Marietta, Samar and Sahara hid behind the door. They forgot to close the main door of the room. Mr. Swang was going into his room. And that secret room was exactly next to his room. While he was going, he saw that the door of the second room was open. He felt a mini heart attack. He hurriedly went inside the room. Samar, Sahara and Marietta got scared. But Mr. Swang didn't know that three people were hidden in the room. He went to the secret door and started checking the door properly.

"Now, what will happen? If he finds out, everything will be annihilated." Marietta said.

"Don't worry, I have a plan." Samar said. "Marietta, you go out of the room slowly and come again as if you are coming right now and then distract him. Next,I will handle it."

Marietta did as Samar said. Mr. Swang was about to open the secret door when suddenly Marietta came in the room and said,

"Mr. Swang " Marietta called him. He quickly took his hand back from the secret door and looked back. "Some people have come to meet you. And they are claiming that this party is illegal. Hurry up, otherwise they will get angry." Marietta said.

Mr. Swang thought that "Illegal party? Who will be these people?"

Then he again turned towards the secret door and looked at the door. He thought that 'I should handle those people first.' And he went from there.

In between this time, Samar sent a message to Sid and alerted him to do it fast. Sid read the message. Sid and Ruhi were right about the key that this key belongs to the treasure. Ruhi unlocked the treasure with the help of the key. They opened it. Then the bright shine came out of the chest. Seeing this shine, their eyes get closed. Then they slowly opened their eyes and looked at the treasure. There was a Crystal Pot, which was shining. Then Ruhi carefully lifted the Crystal Pot in her hand and they both escaped from there. They went upstairs and closed the door of the secret room. On the other side, Mr. Swang went down to meet those strangers as Marietta said. He got shocked and angry because no one had come to meet him. He thought that,

"That girl misled me. Something is wrong." While he was thinking about this, suddenly a light flashed in his mind, "Oh no, My Crystal Pot. That girl was also roaming around that room. I have to go and check."

Mr. Swang ran and while he was running to go to his secret room he saw from a distance that Samar, Ruhi, Sahara and Marietta were standing outside the room, Ruhi held the Crystal Pot in her hand and Sid was closing the door of his secret room.

"Hey, wait...where are you taking my Crystal Pot. Stop, otherwise I will kill you all." Mr. Swang yelled at them and ran to catch them.

"Guys, let's go, run fast." Samar said.

Mr. Swang pulled the knife out of his blazer and ran behind them. He wanted his Crystal Pot back anyhow.

"Jenny...Sia..., quickly run from here." Samar shouted.

Jenny and Sia did not know what had happened. They just ran because Samar said. Mr. Swang called his men to catch them. Mr. Swang and his men started chasing them. He was continuously chasing them to get back his Crystal Pot. Then suddenly Ruhi's gaze went to the Crystal Pot, which she held in her hand. Then, she thought that this was the only thing that could help them.

"Oh Crystal, Please help us to escape from Mr. Swang's eyes." And after saying this she opened the cap of that Crystal Pot.

Then all of sudden they all disappeared and reached in the middle of the forest. That forest was so beautiful and attractive as if it was a heaven.

CHAPTER FIVE

The mysterious girl Ruhi's secret out

Everybody saw towards the Crystal Pot. Crystal Pot was looking so beautiful and it was shining as if the Sun and the Moon were shining. They were all watching continuously. They could not take their eyes off the Crystal Pot.

"Wow!" Everyone was amazed after seeing the Crystal Pot.

"This is amazing! I'm so glad that I'm alive to see this." Jenny said impressively.

"Even I'm so amazed with the Crystal Pot. I never thought this kind of thing could be true." Samar said.

"Okay, we have got the Crystal Pot. But, now what? Mr. Swang will not spare us so easily." Marietta said.

Ruhi looked at Sahara with sad eyes and nodded her head and Sahara nodded too. They both wanted to say something to the other ones.

"We want to tell you something. We have kept one secret from you all since the day we met." Sahara said with a serious face.

"What?" Marietta asked and she was looking confident that something was wrong, because she had doubts about Ruhi from the beginning.

"I will tell you everything. First, you have to come with me to my house. That is the only place from where I can go on my own way." Ruhi said.

"Your way? What do you mean?" Sid asked Ruhi.

She looked into his eyes and said, "Come with me."

They all agreed and went to the haunted house. When they opened the main door of the haunted house, they saw Mr. Swang, sitting on the chair. They were all shocked.

"Welcome, my children, come. I have been waiting for you all for the last one hour." Mr. Swang said and smiled at them.

They all tried to escape but Mr. Swang's men had closed the door and stood around them with the guns in their hands. They were all scared.

"No, no...My dear children you all can't go outside the house without returning my Crystal Pot." Mr. Swang said, gritting his teeth. "Give it back to me, damn it." He yelled at them furiously.

"Mr. Swang, Don't even try to think about this Pot. This Pot was made to help people but you stole this from us and misused it. Do not forget that Crystal Pot is still in my hands. I can do anything with you." Ruhi said.

He suddenly looked at Ruhi with suspicious eyes because she said that Mr. Swang stole Crystal Pot from her. He fell into deep thought. He thought that,

'Is she the same girl whomI killed long years ago? But how is that possible? I had killed her with my own hands. How can she be alive?' He got a little scared. Later he took a deep breath. He tried to show himself strong and said,

"Oh, so you're the one whom I killed. You are still alive."

The other people who stood beside her got surprised and looked at her with big panicked eyes.

"See, I told you that something is wrong." Marietta whispered to Samar. "Now I'm a little confused. Is she alive or dead? I mean Is she a normal person like us or is she a spirit?" she rolled her eyes.

"Something is wrong, that's why she is staying in this haunted house. Otherwise, no one could dare to stay here." Marietta murmured.

"I will clear your doubt, Marietta." Ruhi turned her head slightly towards Marietta. "Trust me I'm not a bad girl." She heard Marietta's babbling.

Ruhi's throat filled with the flood of tears and she said, "Whatever I am today only because of this evil man who killed me ruthlessly." She pointed her finger at Mr. Swang. "I didn't want to be like this, but I became. I fought until the last breath. At last my breath flew. Now I'm not going to spare him. Because the water has gone over the head." A flame of fire appeared in her eyes.

She looked angrily at Mr. Swang and she put hand on Crystal Pot and said, "Oh Crystal, show him the door of hell." And she was going to open the cap of Crystal Pot.

Mr. Swang got scared and said in panic, "No...No...Don't open the cap. I'm admitting my crime. I killed you in this house. Because I wanted to be a king where your grandfather had positioned. I wanted to keep people under me and wanted to make them my slaves. That's why I stole the Crystal Pot from you. However, you were not ready to give me that. And because of that I had to kill you. I'm sorry, Please don't kill me."

However, the pot of his sin was filled. Finally, Ruhi opened the cap and suddenly a shining ray came out of the Crystal Pot and spread all around. Then all of sudden the things that were there started flying and fell with full force on Mr. Swang. Because of the hit, he fell down on the ground. He was trying too hard to save himself. He ran towards the main door but the door was closed. Therefore, he started running towards the stairs. But, all the things were falling him down. He tried again and again but he failed. At last, he gave up and died. His men fled from there. After his death, Ruhi took a deep breath and looked around to her friends. She saw that everyone except Marietta, Sid and Samar were staring at her with fear and many questions were in their eyes.

"I was right about you. You're not a normal girl. I was sceptical of you from the beginning." Marietta said.

"So, the story you told us about the girl, whom Mr. Swang had killed, that was you, am I right?" Samar asked.

"Yes. That's me." Ruhi replied.

"Oh my God" Jenny got scared and took a step back. "It means she is dead." She babbled.

All were looking at her with suspicion.

"Don't be scared. As I said before, I'm not a bad girl. And I'm really sorry guys, I used you all for my personal purpose." Ruhi said politely.

"Just sit and listen to me carefully. I will tell you everything. I'm not here to hurt you all. Trust me." Ruhi added.

Was Ruhi Alive or Dead?

"Now, it's time to reveal the whole truth." Ruhi looked at Sahara and said. Sahara also nodded her head and agreed with Ruhi's decision.

"Yes, it's true that Mr. Swang had killed me. I'm not alive. The girl standing in front of you is not a normal girl. I'm a pure spirit." Ruhi said to all with intense eyes.

Everyone got scared. Jenny held Samar's hand because of the fear. All began to look at her with wide eyes.

"Now, I'm going to open the first page of my life. I belonged to a royal family. My grandfather was a very kind person. He could not see anyone in a bad condition. For that, he used Crystal Pot to help needy people. Then he handed over this Crystal Pot to my mom and he passed away. Then my Mom repeated the same ritual and handed over the Crystal Pot to me, and she died. I became an orphan at a very early age. I tried my best to protect it. But, that evil man snatched a Crystal Pot from me and killed me. He stabbed my stomach three times. He was a heartless man. I was just a 20 years old girl. He didn't even think at least once before hurting me." Ruhi said. Her eyes were filled with tears and heart was filled with pain.

"I can feel your pain. But, What was our role in your story? Why did we meet? Why did you choose us to help you?" Marietta asked without any fear or hesitation.

Then Ruhi took a deep breath and swallowed her emotion and made herself mentally stable and said, "That's my next page which I'm going to turn now. First, I saw Marietta and Samar standing outside the haunted house on the day of Sia's birthday. You both were talking about this house and I was listening to you both carefully. Then you both left and I randomly followed you. Because I was looking for such people who can help me to find my Crystal Pot. However, I found no one so courageous like you guys. Later, you both went to Sia's birthday party and I followed you to the party. While you were all talking about your close and strong friendship, I was standing behind the pillar and secretly listening to you all and watching you all too. At that time, I realized that you were the only people who could help me. Your friendship bond was so strong that I got convinced that all of you could do this courageous work. "

"So, when did you leave the party?" Sia asked.

"When you were all left then." Ruhi replied.

"There is a distance of about 5 kilometers between the party place and this house. So, how did you get here so quickly? Because I remember the first time we officially met here, outside the haunted house." Sia said.

"I think you forgot what I said a while ago that I'm a spirit. I can reach anywhere in a blink of an eye." Ruhi said.

"Oh yes! I had actually forgotten." Sia said.

"At that time I was confident that all of you would help me. That's why I took a lift from you. Sid was looking interested in me, that's why just to clear Marietta and Samar's doubt, I again took a lift from Sid on the next morning. And I came to the same restaurant and called my cousin Sahara there. Then in the restaurant you were all listening to my and Sahara's conversation. That's why Sahara talked about such things, that I always helped her, and all. Then you all started believing in me. But, Marietta was still looking at me suspiciously. But, the rest ones had faith on me and at that time that was enough for me." Ruhi said further.

"Then what about your unconsciousness in the middle of the road?" Sid wanted an explanation.

"That was also part of my plan. Because that was the time to get the Crystal Pot back. That's why me and Sahara made a plan and that doctor was also a part of my plan." Ruhi said.

"Later, I followed Sid and I found out that Sid was going somewhere and again he was going to use the same road. That's why I called Ruhi and told her to be ready." Sahara added.

"Then I went on the road and slept in the middle of the road. Later, Sid saw me and got worried for me. Further you all know what happened." Ruhi explained the whole truth.

"I have one more confusion that souls never bleed and your forehead was bleeding that day. How is that possible?" Jenny asked nervously.

"That was a Red colour. Fortunately, I could touch things." Ruhi smiled and said.

"All the things I was doing step by step according to my planning. I don't know when I started feeling a strong bond with you all. Hence, I was feeling bad that I was using you all for my own purpose. Please accept my apology. I'm extremely sorry." Ruhi apologised.

"It's okay, Ruhi. You did all those things for a good purpose. We are glad that we did some good deeds because of you." Marietta said politely

All began to look at the Marietta. Because she had never trusted Ruhi. But, now she was the only one who was consoling Ruhi.

"Why are you all looking at me like this? Oh, come on! I'm not as bad as you all are thinking." Marietta said.

"Thank you, Marietta. I'm glad that I earned your trust and friendship." Ruhi smiled and said. "But, I think our friendship is not for a long period." Ruhi said sadly.

"Why?" Sid asked.

"My time is over. I was here only for this Crystal Pot. Now my mission is over. So, I have to go now." Ruhi said.

"Where will you go?" Sia asked.

"To my Home... 'Heaven'. I'm not a normal girl as you are. I'm a pure soul who came here to take my Crystal Pot back. I'm glad that I met you." Everyone's faces turned sad.

"And yes of course, I remember my promise that I will give you this Crystal Pot to fulfil one of your wishes. Whatever you want, tell your wish to Crystal Pot." Ruhi said.

Then they all looked at Crystal Pot. Sid was very attached to Ruhi. He didn't feel good that Ruhi was leaving him forever. Therefore, the other friends put that Crystal Pot in front of Sid.

"I think you should ask for something from Crystal Pot. Because I have what I want." Marietta said.

Jenny and Sia also came forward and said, "We also have everything. We want nothing."

Then Samar also said the same thing.

Ruhi saw this beautiful moment and she smiled at them. Sid got a little emotional and he looked at each of them. He didn't tell them anything , but he was thankful for that.

Then Sid came forward and took Crystal Pot in his hands. He expressed his desire in front of the Crystal Pot. Then, he opened the cap of the Crystal Pot. Do you know what his desire was? Let me tell you.With the tears in his eyes he said to Crystal Pot that,

"Ruhi.., I want Ruhi back."

Ruhi jerked her head and said,

"That's impossible! I'm not alive. You know that."

The Crystal Pot disappeared. His wish remained unfulfilled. It is not possible to bring a dead person back to life. Ruhi got emotional. She took a deep breath and took a step back. Then shining rays came and fell on Ruhi. That shine was so bright that everyone's eyes got closed. But, Sid managed to keep his eyes open and he brought his hand forward to stop her. But, now it was too late, the shining light came and took Ruhi with him. Later the other ones opened their eyes and they found that Ruhi was not there.

"Where is Ruhi?" Sia asked.

"She's gone." Sid said in a deep voice, he remained silent for a few seconds, and then said again, "Forever."

Everybody became upset, but Sid was shocked.

"That's okay, we wished for the wrong thing. How can it be possible that one dead person will come back?" Samar said.

Samar put his hand on Sid's shoulder. He took him away from the haunted house. Everyone went home. Then, their normal life resumed. Sid was a little upset. But, his friends thought that time will heal him soon.

The next day Sid was going to BG's restaurant. He sat in the car and started driving the car. On the way a haunted house came. And He saw that one girl was standing next to the haunted house. Sid instantly stopped the car. He thought that it might be a Ruhi. He smiled and stepped out from the car hurriedly. He went to her and said with lots of hope in his heart.

"Excuse me!"

She turned back. That girl wasn't Ruhi. She was someone else. Sid looked at her and lost in his thoughts.

"Excuse me, I'm talking to you." She waved her hand on Sid's face because he was lost somewhere.

"Yes...Yes..." He stammered. "Who are you?" He asked her.

She smiled and said, "That doesn't matter." She looked at the other side of house and said,

"Someone is waiting for you there." She pointed her finger.

Sid saw and went there. That girl giggled. There was no one there. He went back to tell her that no one was there. But that girl was not there either. Sid was surprised.

"What's happening with me?" He shook his head and went back to his car. Then suddenly he heard someone's voice. The voice was coming from the haunted house. He followed the voice. He entered the house. He was amazed to see the person standing in front of him. For a few moments, he stood like an idol and stared at that person.

"I'm back." Sid heard those words and the beautiful smile came on his face. I know you must have realized who came back.Obviously Ruhi.

"This time I came here to stay forever." She said in her beautiful voice. "God gave me the second chance. Your wish came true."

"Welcome back, Ruhi!" Sid said with lots of happiness.

He then took her to meet his other friends. Everyone was surprised and happy seeing Ruhi. However, the haunted house was no longer a haunted house. It became a normal house.

"It doesn't matter how much bad intentions try to stop you, Goodness never dies." Marietta said

"All's well that ends well." Jenny said happily.

Made in the USA
Monee, IL
07 July 2026

56550095R00022